Access To Print

Put Beginning Readers on the Right Track with
ALL ABOARD READING™

The All Aboard Reading series is especially designed for beginning readers. Written by noted authors and illustrated in full color, these are books that children really want to read—books to excite their imagination, expand their interests, make them laugh, and support their feelings. With fiction and nonfiction stories that are high interest and curriculum-related, All Aboard Reading books offer something for every young reader. And with four different reading levels, the All Aboard Reading series lets you choose which books are most appropriate for your children and their growing abilities.

Picture Readers
Picture Readers have super-simple texts, with many nouns appearing as rebus pictures. At the end of each book are 24 flash cards—on one side is a rebus picture; on the other side is the written-out word.

Station Stop 1
Station Stop 1 books are best for children who have just begun to read. Simple words and big type make these early reading experiences more comfortable. Picture clues help children to figure out the words on the page. Lots of repetition throughout the text helps children to predict the next word or phrase—an essential step in developing word recognition.

Station Stop 2
Station Stop 2 books are written specifically for children who are reading with help. Short sentences make it easier for early readers to understand what they are reading. Simple plots and simple dialogue help children with reading comprehension.

Station Stop 3
Station Stop 3 books are perfect for children who are reading alone. With longer text and harder words, these books appeal to children who have mastered basic reading skills. More complex stories captivate children who are ready for more challenging books.

In addition to All Aboard Reading books, look for All Aboard Math Readers™ (fiction stories that teach math concepts children are learning in school) and All Aboard Science Readers™ (nonfiction books that explore the most fascinating science topics in age-appropriate language).

All Aboard for happy reading!

Special thanks to Paul Dyer Photography.

Library of Congress Cataloging-in-Publication Data

Moffatt, Judith.
   Who stole the cookies? / by Judith Moffatt.
     p.   cm. — (All aboard reading. Level 1)
   Summary: Each in a series of animals denies taking the cookies,
but the true thief turns up in a cave.
    [1. Cookies—Fiction. 2. Animals—Fiction. 3. Stories in rhyme.]
    I. Title. II. Series.
  PZ8.3.M716Wh 1996
  [E]—dc20 95-20847   CIP   AC

ISBN 0-448-41127-X   2004 Printing

For Morgan, Raisin, Minky, and Budgie

Who Stole the COOKIES?

By Judith Moffatt

Grosset & Dunlap • New York

Who stole the cookies
from the cookie jar?

I think Cat
stole the cookies
from the
cookie jar.

5

Who, me?

Yes, you.

Not me.

Then who?

I think Puppy
stole the cookies
from the cookie jar.

Who, me?

Yes, you.

Not me.

10

Then who?

I think Mouse
stole the cookies
from the cookie jar.

Who, me?

No siree.

Come along.

Follow me.

DEL NORTE
ELEMENTARY LIBRARY

I think Squirrel
stole the cookies
from the cookie jar.

Who, me,
did you say?
Not me. No way!

I think Turtle
stole the cookies
from the cookie jar.

Oh, no! Not true!
But here is a clue.

You will find
the thief in there!
Look in the cave
if you dare!

Bear stole the cookies
from the cookie jar!

I'm a very sorry bear.
But it's so hard
to share.

26

Don't cry.

I'll tell you why.

27

Everybody follow me!

We'll bake more cookies, .
one, two, three!

Yum!

Let's have some.